Aziza's
·Secret Fairy·
Door
and the
Birthday Present Disaster

Other books by Lola Morayo

Aziza's Secret Fairy Door

*Aziza's Secret Fairy Door and the
Ice Cat Mystery*

Coming soon!

*Aziza's Secret Fairy Door
and the Mermaid's Treasure*

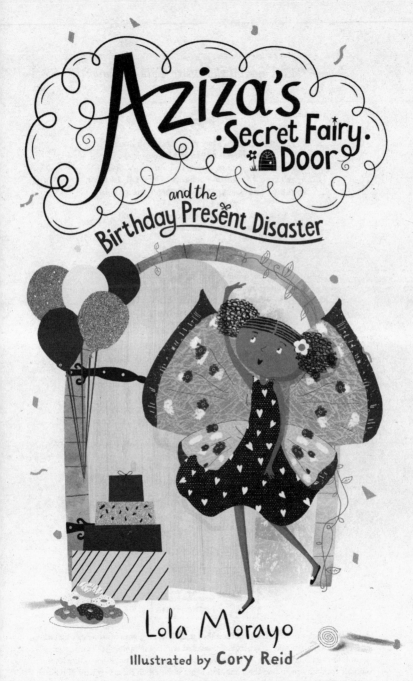

Aziza's
·Secret Fairy·
Door
and the
Birthday Present Disaster

Lola Morayo

Illustrated by Cory Reid

MACMILLAN CHILDREN'S BOOKS

With special thanks to Tọ́lá Okogwu

Published 2022 by Macmillan Children's Books
an imprint of Pan Macmillan
The Smithson, 6 Briset Street, London EC1M 5NR
EU representative: Macmillan Publishers Ireland Ltd, 1st Floor,
The Liffey Trust Centre, 117–126 Sheriff Street Upper
Dublin 1, D01 YC43
Associated companies throughout the world
www.panmacmillan.com

ISBN 978-1-5290-6397-4

3 5 7 9 8 6 4 2

A CIP catalogue record for this book is available from the British Library.

Printed and bound by CPI Group (UK) Ltd, Croydon CR0 4YY

To Folu and Seye.

Thank you for your support.

T. O.

For class 1 Oak – you are magic!

Thanks for the sparkle Mr Mitcham and Mrs Henwood.

J. R.

I love you little Mum

C. R.

Chapter 1

'I'm running out of time,' Aziza sighed as she stared down at the piles of multicoloured paper and the half-completed invitations to her brother Otis's surprise birthday party. The party she was organizing . . .

well, *trying* to anyway.

Aziza picked up an invitation and stared at the picture of Jamal Justice on the front. Otis loved the superhero star of their parents' graphic novels, which was why he was the

perfect theme for the party, but there just didn't seem to be enough time to get everything done. The party was just a week away.

Aziza blew out a frustrated breath. *It's got to be special, but I don't know what to do first.*

'Hey, Zizzles,' a voice called out, and Aziza quickly stuffed the invitations underneath some nearby sugar paper. But it was just her parents. Otis was nowhere to be seen.

'How are you getting on with the party planning?' her dad asked, coming into the living room.

'I'm not,' Aziza muttered. 'I still haven't finished the invitations.' She waved towards the pile on the floor. 'I still need to work out the menu,' she continued, her voice getting squeaky, 'and decide what music to play.'

Mum winced, knelt and placed a finger

under Aziza's chin, tilting her face up.

'I know it was your idea to give Otis a surprise party but we are here to help, you know. You don't have to do this by yourself.'

'I used to be a DJ. I could help pick the songs?' Dad offered with a grin.

'I need songs from this century, Dad,' Aziza replied. She shook her head. 'I can do it. I *want* to do it.'

'OK, Zizzles,' Dad said. 'Just remember, the smartest people ask for help.'

Mum gave Aziza's nose an affectionate tap before she and Dad left the room.

Aziza stared after them. *Maybe I could get them to help with the cutting? Or the gluing? Or writing out the——*

Otis whizzed into the room at full speed. 'Yo, Zizi. Want to play pirate fairies?'

Aziza shook her head and started packing up the party stuff so Otis wouldn't see.

'I can't, I'm busy.' Aziza's voice wobbled. Seeing him just made her even more worried that she was going to mess his party up.

Her brother peered at her. 'What's wrong? You look just like you did when I buried your fairy doll in the sandpit . . .

Then forgot where I put her.'

Otis's words were the final straw, especially as she couldn't actually tell him anything without ruining his birthday surprise.

'Just leave me alone.' Aziza leapt up from the carpet. She dashed past a startled Otis and headed straight for her bedroom. She shut the door, grabbed her Fairy Power cushion from her bed and gave it a hug.

Somehow the soft plush made her feel a bit better.

There was a rattling sound from the windowsill. Aziza's gaze went to the wooden fairy door that stood there – it was sparkling.

Aziza gasped as a cute ribbon magically unfurled around the edges of the door and tied itself in a messy bow. It could only mean one thing. *I'm going back to the magical kingdom of Shimmerton!*

Tingling with excitement, Aziza moved towards the fairy door. She untied the bow. The ribbon was smooth and soft beneath her fingertips. Next, she gently took hold of the bejewelled doorknob and felt a glowing warmth fill her whole body as the fairy door swung open. Then she was shrinking, and a golden beam of light surrounded her.

Aziza stepped through the door and into a magnificent ballroom. Once it had closed, the fairy door could hardly be noticed in the wall behind her. All around, creatures were dressed in beautiful party clothes and they chattered and giggled. Huge balloons swooped and twirled in the air, lit up by twinkling fairy lights. Bright tapestries covered the walls,

illuminated by big glowing lanterns.

'Where am I?' Aziza whispered. She looked down at herself, curious to see what she would be wearing this time. She gasped at the sight of the beautiful party dress, covered in shining silver hearts that sparkled under all the lights. Her butterfly wings were back too, and Aziza gave them a little flutter.

I'm at a party! Aziza thought with a grin.

Just then, a small bear-like creature in a waistcoat bustled past. He had a clipboard in his hand and a worried frown on his face.

'Tiko!' Aziza called out, happy to see

her little shapeshifting friend. She hadn't recognized him at first with his smart waistcoat on! Tiko looked up and his frown melted away when he spotted Aziza.

'Oh, goodness, I'm so pleased to see you!' he said.

'What's going on?' Aziza asked. 'Where are we?'

'It's Peri's birthday party, and I'm the palace's official party planner,' Tiko replied. 'Peri wanted to organize the party without her parents' help but I'm allowed to assist.'

Aziza grinned at him, thinking how funny

it was that her friends had been organizing a party while she'd been doing the same thing at home for Otis. 'I bet you're doing an amazing job.'

'I hope so!' Tiko waved the clipboard about. 'We promised the king and queen we'd throw the best royal party ever!'

'Well, everyone looks like they're having a great time!' Aziza said looking at the party guests. 'Besides, I'm here now and I can help.'

Tiko nodded. 'I'm so glad you *are* here. We weren't sure how to get hold of you.' Then he grinned. 'Good thing that the fairy door always knows what to do.'

Aziza hugged that thought to herself. The door really did know when to bring her to Shimmerton, and with the way time froze at home, she didn't have to hurry back either. Besides, helping to organize a party for Peri might help her with ideas for Otis's party.

'Would you like a drink?' Tiko asked as he led Aziza to a long banquet table, filled with the yummiest looking food and the most colourful drinks.

'Wow, this looks amazing.' Aziza picked up a sparkling pink glass and took a sip. 'It tastes like strawberries and sherbet fizzing inside my mouth.' She giggled. 'It's tickly.'

Tiko looked pleased. 'We have something for everyone. Buttercup slushies for the unicorns. Lime and honeysuckle smoothies for the pixies. I even got a chocolate- and carrot-flavoured milkshake for Mrs Sayeed's son.'

Tiko pointed to a happy looking Almiraj. He wore a party hat on top of his horn and his bunny ears stood up in delight at his drink.

Everyone looked as if they were having fun and Aziza spotted an older fairy with swan-like feathers, a neat moustache and a crown on his head. Beside him was a fairy in silk robes with long flowing dark hair and a glittering headdress. They were busy greeting guests as they entered. *They must be the king and queen,* Aziza thought. *Peri's parents. But where is their daughter?*

'Where's Peri?' Aziza asked.

'In her room, but she should *really* be down by now.' Tiko looked up at a big golden clock on the wall. 'Don't suppose you could get her? She'll be so excited to see you.'

Before Aziza could reply, he reeled off a series of directions. 'Oh, and tell her not to forget the presents,' Tiko added before bustling away again.

Forget the presents? Aziza thought in

confusion. It didn't make much sense to her. Surely Peri wouldn't have been given her presents yet? She shrugged and set off to find her friend.

Outside the ballroom, Aziza walked along the hallway lined with golden scalloped tiles and jewelled borders just like Tiko told her. She'd never seen anything so beautiful, until she turned right and caught a glimpse of the staircase. It was golden too!

'Glittersticks,' Aziza breathed in awe.

The large staircase glimmered brightly as it spiralled upwards. A red velvet carpet ran

up the centre. As Aziza climbed the stairs, she felt like a princess in her very own fairy tale. Right down to the special dress.

At the top of the stairs, Aziza stopped, suddenly unsure which way led to Peri's room. There were so many doors. *Which one was the right one? I can't remember!*

Chapter 2

Aziza stared at each of the doors and noticed that one had a garland of conkers, acorns and pine cones hanging from the doorknob. She smiled and knocked on that door.

'Come in,' said a familiar voice.

I knew it. Aziza opened the door and stepped into the room. The walls were painted in a sunny yellow. In the middle of the room sat a huge four-poster bed draped in gauzy sheer fabric that was shot through with azure and emerald threads. The room was beautiful . . . and it was a complete mess. There were clothes everywhere and Peri was staring at a pile of dresses at her feet.

'Aziza!' squealed Peri when she caught

sight of her friend. 'You're here!'

Peri's feathered wings fluttered in delight as she gave Aziza a big hug.

'The fairy door called me,' Aziza replied.

Peri nodded. 'I told Tiko it would, but he does like to worry.'

'He's worried now actually.' Aziza said. 'He reckons you're late.'

'I'm completely stuck.' Peri blew a breath of frustration. 'I can't find the right outfit.'

Aziza raised an eyebrow and stared at the floor strewn with clothes. 'Maybe it's because they're all on the floor?'

Peri gave her a friendly shove. 'I'm being

serious. Mrs Hattie, our housekeeper, laid out all these princess-perfect party dresses but that's not me . . . you know?'

Aziza did know. Peri liked shorts and T-shirts, preferably torn or muddy, so she could get on with her tree climbing.

'But then I want everything to be perfect today,' Peri muttered. 'It's the first party I've been in charge of and I don't want to let Mum and Dad down. Princesses have to be able to know how to throw a party. It's in the job description.'

'You won't let anyone down.' Aziza

assured her. 'You and Tiko have done an amazing job.'

'Tiko's been amazing,' Peri replied. 'I hope it's not been too much for him.'

Aziza shook her head. 'He seems really attached to that clipboard but I'm sure he's fine. Especially once you're *downstairs*.'

'OK, OK.' Peri wrinkled her nose. 'But what am I going to wear?'

Aziza scanned the pile of clothes littering the ground. 'How about this one?' she said picking up a pretty dress with a pattern woven with golden and amber thread. The design looked like shimmery tree branches. *Just like the trees Peri likes to climb.*

'It's perfect,' sighed Peri. 'How did you know?'

'It just felt very you,' Aziza replied with a grin.

Peri grabbed the dress and quickly put it on. She finished the look with a beautiful tiara.

'You look amazing,' Aziza said. 'Let's go. Hang on. Tiko said something about the . . . presents?'

'Gah! The presents!' Peri ran to her wardrobe and frantically began rummaging inside. More clothes landed on the floor. She dashed to her bed next and began flinging the remaining cushions from it.

Her room was getting messier by the second and Aziza was feeling properly confused.

'They're not here.' Peri threw her hands up in the air. 'I can't find the presents for my guests.'

Aziza frowned back. 'Don't you mean presents for you?'

Peri looked up from the chest she was now rummaging through. 'Why would I be getting presents?'

'It's your birthday. Everyone gets *you* presents.'

Peri shut the chest with a loud thump. 'Not in Shimmerton. Here, the birthday person gets presents for everyone else.' Then she put her hands on her hips. 'But I can't find them, they've gone missing!' She scrubbed a hand over her face. 'This is terrible,' she wailed.

'I was really looking forward to seeing everyone's smiles when they opened them. Especially Tiko. He's so tricky to buy stuff for.'

Aziza put a hand on her shoulder. 'I'm sure he won't mind.'

Peri shook her head. 'You don't understand. My parents will be so disappointed. I'm a princess, I'm supposed to be organized.'

'OK, look. Maybe someone took them down already?' Aziza soothed. 'Let's go down to the party, I'm sure they'll turn up.'

Peri nodded. 'OK, but we should check

all the other bedrooms first.'

So, they did, but there was no sign of the presents anywhere and Aziza never wanted to see a four-poster bed again. There had been a lot of bedrooms. The girls headed back down the gleaming staircase and into the ballroom.

'Peri! My darling,' cooed a gentle voice as soon as they entered. 'You look wonderful. That dress really suits you!'

It was the queen. Her beautiful robes glittered almost as much as her golden headdress. Next to her was the king. A grin

31

lit up his handsome face.

'Mum, Dad, this is Aziza.' Peri said eagerly.

The king smiled kindly at Aziza.

'What a pleasure to finally meet you,' the queen replied. 'We've heard so much about you.'

Before Aziza could reply, a tall fairy butler wearing a long black coat and white gloves scurried forwards and bowed.

'Your Highnesses,' he said, looking frazzled. 'The royal family from Glimmershire has arrived. They are demanding an audience with you!'

'We'd better say hello,' the queen replied with a sigh. 'You know how easily offended people from Glimmershire can get.'

'I hope we can speak properly later,' the king said to Aziza with an apologetic smile.

Aziza nodded back and, together, the king and queen strode off.

'I should really go with them,' Peri said anxiously, watching her parents walk away.

'Don't worry, I'll hunt down the presents.' Aziza winked. 'You go do your princess thing.'

Peri smiled at Aziza gratefully then hurried after them.

I wonder where Tiko is? Aziza thought. *He'll be able to help me track down those presents.* She quickly scanned the ballroom, but instead of Tiko's friendly furry face, she found three giggling ones instead. Sat in a circle were Kendra, Felly and Noon. *The Gigglers*, Aziza thought. *Great*. What mischief were they up to this time?

'Pass it already,' demanded Kendra.

The blue-haired fairy lunged for the small brightly wrapped parcel in Noon's hands.

'I just got it,' Noon cried as she dodged Kendra's grabbing hands. Her pink candyfloss curls bounced in indignation. 'Felly was hogging it.'

'I did not!' Felly spluttered as her moth
wings flapped angrily.

Beside them sat a girl in the most amazing
rainbow dress. The colours seemed to burst
from it in a kaleidoscope of hues. Her
multicoloured braids hung down her back,

but her hands were empty. She didn't seem to be enjoying the game of pass the parcel *at all*.

Those Gigglers, thought Aziza. *Always a drama*. She watched as the music played again and the parcel was passed from girl to girl. Each time Kendra got it, she held onto it for far too long and the girl in the rainbow dress got more upset. The music stopped again and Kendra still had the parcel. The girl with the rainbow braids got up to leave. The Gigglers didn't even notice, but Aziza did.

She rushed towards the girl. 'Are you all right?'

The girl looked startled. 'Nothing is going right,' she whispered. 'I can't even play pass the parcel correctly.'

Aziza sighed. 'That wasn't your fault. It's those Gigglers not sharing . . . as usual.'

But the girl didn't seem to be listening.

'I just need to fix things. No more wonkiness. No more fading,' she muttered before walking away, her head bent low.

Aziza went to chase after her but Kendra had spotted her and fluttered to her side. 'Should have known you'd turn up,' Kendra said sourly.

'Nice to see you too, Kendra,' Aziza replied.

'You weren't being very nice to that girl.'

'Who . . . Resa?' Kendra scoffed. 'Some people can't take a joke.'

Aziza put her hands on her hips. 'I don't think hogging the parcel is very funny.'

'That's because you can't take a joke either,' Kendra said. 'Besides, Resa is *way* too sensitive. We would have passed the parcel eventually.'

'Yeah,' Felly and Noon shouted over. 'Eventually.'

All three Gigglers burst out giggling.

Aziza eyed the Gigglers with narrowed eyes. *They wouldn't have taken the presents for the guests . . . would they?* She quickly dismissed the idea. Sure, the Gigglers liked to 'borrow' things that didn't belong to them but if they'd taken the presents, they wouldn't still be here. *There has to be another explanation for where the presents went.*

Aziza left the giggling trio to look for Tiko. She scanned the ballroom for presents at the same time. No presents but she spotted Tiko by the music system. It looked a bit like a church organ but with lots of flashing buttons.

'Tiko, I need to tell you about the presents. They are mi—'

'Can't talk right now,' he interrupted. 'I'm in charge of the music for all the games and there are so many buttons.'

Aziza waited but Tiko couldn't seem to decide which button to press next.

'We're waiting,' Kendra called out in an impatient voice.

Tiko stopped the music and Noon eagerly ripped into the parcel now in her hands. After a moment, Tiko restarted it again.

'Right, what were you saying about

presents?' Tiko yelled over the noise.

'The presents. They are missing!' Aziza yelled back.

Tiko blinked then suddenly he began to shake, before disappearing in a flash of sparkles. In his place was a giant tortoise, who had retreated into its shell.

'Oi!' Kendra yelled. 'We can't have a tortoise on the music. They're way too slow.'

Aziza quickly stopped and then restarted the music, then turned back to the giant shell.

'Tiko?' she whispered. 'Come out will you?'

'Gah!' replied Tiko. Ever so slowly, his wrinkled head popped out of the shell. 'This . . . is . . . a . . . disaster,' he said very slowly. 'If . . . we . . . don't . . . find . . . the . . . presents . . . the . . . party . . . will . . . be . . . ruined.'

'Don't worry, I'm on it,' Aziza assured him. 'I'll find them. You just keep the party going.'

Tiko nodded, slowly, but he didn't look very convinced. Aziza gave his shell a small pat, then made her way out of the ballroom.

Chapter 3

'Right.' Aziza smoothed down her party dress. 'Time to find those presents. I just have to widen the search.' Following the golden hallway again, Aziza found herself in the kitchens. Pixies and brownies bustled around an electric cauldron that bubbled away. It smelled delicious, but there were still no presents. Next, she tried the drawing room, where a magical ping-pong table invited her to play. Aziza declined politely.

There are just too many rooms and too many people, Aziza realized as she searched first the parlour, then a library. *The presents could be anywhere*, she thought as she entered the next room. Then her eyes widened as she spotted a length of red carpet that led to a giant golden throne with two seats. *Woah! I'm in the throne room*, she thought, walking forwards.

The throne was so big, it needed three
steps just to climb it. Aziza looked around
quickly then, unable to help herself, she lifted

her foot towards the first step.

But the sound of voices next door stopped her.

'It's probably not allowed,' Aziza whispered to herself. 'And you've got presents to find!'

Instead, she quickly searched the throne room for the missing presents, but once again, found nothing. The voices next door kept getting louder. And there seemed to be some kind of discussion about running chairs?

Aziza went to investigate and found herself in a banqueting hall, full of chairs and a table that looked long enough to fit her whole class. She also found all the guests from the party in there, including Peri and Tiko, who was back to his normal self.

'Please tell me you found the presents,' Peri cried anxiously. 'I feel so bad you're missing the party!'

Aziza smiled reassuringly. 'I'm still

searching for the presents and don't worry about me missing out. It's fun to check out the palace.'

Tiko tapped his clipboard. 'Swifty chairs is about to start. I brought everyone in here so we can play it properly. We don't want any bumped heads.'

'Swifty chairs?' Aziza replied.

Peri grinned. 'It's so much fun. The chairs are magical and you have to chase them down if you want a seat.'

The guests began to take their seats and Peri's grin turned into a frown.

'Hold on. Shouldn't there be more people?'

Aziza followed her gaze and found she was right. Three chairs were empty. *First the presents go missing, now the guests*, Aziza thought perplexed. *What's going on?*

Tiko waved his clipboard anxiously. 'Everyone has arrived. I ticked them off myself.' He pointed at the list of names and sure enough, there was a tick by each one. 'I checked it carefully and made sure the right number of chairs were put out.'

Aziza patted her distraught friend. 'I'm sure you did.' She turned to Peri. 'Do you remember who's missing?'

Peri's forehead creased in concentration. 'I'm not sure. We invited a lot of people and some are my parents' guests.' She quickly scanned the room again. 'I can only see Fern Bracken,' Peri said pointing to a small unicorn in a purple tank top. 'Finn Bracken should be here too.'

'Are they Mr Bracken's kids?' Aziza asked curiously. Fern and Finn had the same surname as the unicorn who owned Shimmerton's toy store.

Peri shook her head. 'His niece and nephew.'

Aziza nodded. 'OK, we need to find out if the missing guests are connected to the missing presents. We should make sure 'no one has left the palace.'

'The guards at the palace gates!' Tiko cried excitedly. 'They'll know if anyone has left.'

'Let's go!' Peri said. 'It's not fair to leave this all to Aziza. I'll just tell my parents I'm getting some air.'

The three friends left the banqueting hall swiftly, but they didn't get very far.

'What's that noise?' Aziza asked as they hurried down a hallway.

Tiko and Peri stopped.

'It sounds like —' Tiko's little ears wiggled hard — 'wailing!'

'Oh no, not at my party,' Peri exclaimed. 'I hate the idea of anyone being sad. Do you think it might be Finn?'

For a moment Aziza remembered the sad expression of the girl with the rainbow braids. She hoped she was all right.

They followed the sound of wailing to a closed door.

'It's one of the bathrooms,' Peri said, knocking. 'Finn, are you in there? Are you OK?'

An unhappy-looking unicorn opened the door. He looked a bit green. 'I did something terrible,' moaned Finn.

'What happened?' Aziza asked urgently. 'Is it to do with the presents?'

'No, I ate too many clover crisps,' gulped Finn. 'Even though Uncle warned me and now I feel awful.' Finn rubbed his tummy. 'What presents?'

Aziza smiled in relief. While she felt sorry for Finn, she was also really glad that he had nothing to do with the missing presents.

'The presents for the guests. I spent ages wrapping them,' Peri whispered almost to herself. 'My parents even let me use magical ribbons for the first time. Just on a few of the presents though.'

'Magical ribbons?' Aziza asked puzzled.

Finn looked wistful. 'Magical ribbons are the best. They're famous for inspiring joy and creativity.'

'And they're super rare too,' Tiko said.

Peri nodded. 'That's why I only used them on a few of the gifts.'

There was a gasping noise from the doorway and Aziza whipped round but there was no one there. *Strange*, she thought, before turning back to the others.

'Don't worry,' said Tiko as he patted Peri on the shoulder. 'We'll find the presents.'

'We should probably find someone to take care of Finn first though,' Aziza suggested.

Peri nodded. 'Mrs Hattie, our housekeeper should be around somewhere.'

Together they went in search of her, helping Finn walk along. They found the sphinx folding napkins in the kitchen. Her bird eyes shone with concern when she saw them.

'Whatever is going on?' Mrs Hattie cried. 'Shouldn't you lot be playing swifty chairs?'

'Finn isn't feeling very well,' Tiko replied.

Mrs Hattie bustled forward, her feathered wings flapping as she fussed over the unicorn. 'Come on, dear. Let's get you some water.'

'You haven't seen Peri's presents have you, Mrs Hattie?' Aziza asked.

The sphinx looked up. 'Indeed, I have.
I brought them downstairs earlier and put
them in the throne room.'

Peri straightened in surprise. 'You moved them! Why?'

'Your room is always a mess, your Highness,' Mrs Hattie replied sternly, the hair on her cat-like body bristling. 'I didn't want them getting stepped on like the cupcakes from yesterday's snack time.'

Peri blushed guiltily.

Aziza frowned. 'Well, they're not in the throne room any more. I checked.'

'You don't think they were stolen, do you?' fretted Mrs Hattie. 'No, that can't be right,' she added as she handed Finn a cup of water. 'No one in Shimmerton would do such a thing. It must all just be one big misunderstanding. The palace is just chaos today.'

Aziza hoped that was true. 'We still have two missing people to find,' she said. 'Maybe one of them knows something?'

'You investigate that and I'll send some of the pixies to search the palace for the presents,' Mrs Hattie said.

Aziza, Tiko and Peri said goodbye to Finn and Mrs Hattie, then set off for the palace gates once again. There they found two

straight-backed,

wooden toy soldiers

keeping watch.

'No one has been in

or out since the party

started,' said the first

guard when Aziza asked

him. 'We take our duties

very seriously.'

The second guard suddenly looked uncomfortable. 'We did step out to get some of that delicious carrot and chocolate milkshake.'

'So, someone could have left?' Aziza asked.

The first guard coughed sheepishly. 'I suppose it's possible, but highly unlike—'

'I did see a shifty-looking spider heading for the gardens,' the second guard interrupted eagerly. 'He was holding something.'

'That must be Nansi,' Peri cried in excitement. 'I don't think he was in the banquetting hall now I come to think of it.'

Could he have the presents? Aziza wondered. The trio quickly thanked the guards before rushing off. They had a spider to find!

Chapter 4

They arrived at a building made entirely of glass. It sparkled in the sun and the stained-glass windows shimmered with bursts of fiery colours. Inside, amazing glass archways soared upwards and carved crystal pillars lined the edges and bounced tiny rainbows around the chamber. *The colours are so beautiful,* Aziza thought, but there was no spider or presents in sight.

On they continued with the search. Peri showed Aziza the bubble pool right in the centre of the glasshouse. The bubbles were pink and purple and blue and green and each time one popped they released a little sigh of a song that made Aziza feel relaxed and happy. She kind of wished she could stay but knew they had a spider to find. So they followed a crystal pathway until they reached a sign that said:

You are now entering
the Aloe Garden

The plants in here were large and waxy.

Some rose up into the air and towered over

Aziza and her friends. Their leaves were thick and pointy like star-shaped clusters. It was like walking through a desert oasis.

'Mum likes to make all sorts of creams and gels with the aloe vera,' Peri said proudly. 'She says this stuff is magic.'

They searched through the prickly plants and trees, but still no Nansi. Next, they arrived at a playground with a swing, trampoline and a giant slide shaped like a dragon. Its tongue snaked across the whole playground like the water chutes at Aziza's local swimming pool back at home.

'This is amazing,' Aziza cried, looking up at the tall slide. *It looks really fast.*

'Not so amazing if you have to play on your own,' Peri grumbled. 'It's only fun when your friends come round. Peri plonked herself down on one of the swings. 'This is hopeless. Nansi isn't here either. This is the worst birthday ever.'

Aziza and Tiko stared at each other with concern.

'There's still the maze,' Tiko reassured her. 'He might be there.'

Peri's eyes widened. 'I don't really fancy going to the maze.'

'Why?' Aziza said. 'What's wrong with it?'

'It's enchanted,' Peri whispered. 'The way out changes every single time.' She shook her head. 'Dad realizes it's a terrible idea now but doesn't have the heart to take the maze out.'

Tiko but his lip. 'We should still check there.'

'And with the three of us, I'm sure we'll find our way out!' Aziza said, trying to be encouraging.

They trudged to the maze and soon the side of a solid green hedge towered over them. *Glittersticks! This maze is huge. We don't have time to get lost.*

'I could try shapeshifting into something really tall like a Naga?' Tiko offered.

Aziza and Peri shared a quick look. Tiko was great at shapeshifting but not necessarily into the thing he intended.

'Um . . .' Aziza said.

'Er . . .' Peri added.

It was too late. Tiko shut his eyes and his face got all scrunchy. Aziza held her breath. Suddenly Tiko began to shake, then he disappeared in a shower of sparkles. Tiko had transformed . . . into a giant green serpent.

Aziza and Peri scrambled backwards.

'Tiko?' Aziza's voice was a bit wobbly.

'Yessss,' the serpent hissed in response 'Don't worry, Aziza. It's just me.'

'That's so cool,' Peri said excitedly. 'It's your best transformation yet!'

Tiko grinned, his lips stretching wide over his huge fangs. Then he raised his long neck and peered over the thick hedge wall.

'I can see a path through the maze,' he hissed. 'It goes right through the middle.'

Tiko led the way through the narrow pathways, Aziza and Peri following close behind him. At the centre of the maze, sitting on a wooden bench, was a little boy. A little boy with eight hairy legs. Just like a spider's legs.

'Nansi,' Peri cried in relief. 'We've been looking for you.'

Nansi blinked at Peri, Tiko and Aziza in surprise. 'You have?' he replied. 'Sorry. It was getting a bit loud inside.'

'You didn't like the songs?' Tiko hissed, sounding very put-out.

Nansi stared up at the giant serpent in alarm.

'It's OK,' Aziza said quickly. 'He's harmless.'

'Yessss. Harmlesss,' Tiko hissed, and the next moment he'd transformed back into his usual self. 'I didn't mean to scare you.'

'No problem,' Nansi replied. 'The music was great. I just needed a bit of quiet and I found this maze. I love mazes.' He held up a small glass dome. 'Look, I won this cool snow globe in pass the parcel and it's got a maze inside it.'

78

'Aah,' Tiko said. 'You got the mirror snow globe. It takes whatever elements are around you and mirrors them inside to make up a story.'

'Yeah, I've been watching the story.' Nansi scratched the back of his neck, using three of his legs. 'I must have lost track of the time.'

So that must be what the palace guards saw him carrying, Aziza realized. Which meant they were no closer to finding the missing presents. Aziza looked at her friends and knew they'd realized the same thing.

'We'd better head back inside,' Peri said

with a sigh. 'You'll need to shapeshift again,

Tiko, and lead us out.'

Nansi jumped up. 'I can get us out. I told

you. I love mazes.' Then he hopped off the

bench and scurried through a gap in the

hedge wall. 'Follow me,' he called.

It did not take them long to make their

way out of the maze with Nansi leading the

way. In no time at all, they were back outside the banqueting hall.

'You know you can go to the parlour if you need another break,' Peri told Nansi. 'It's quiet there and I know parties can be a bit full on.'

The spider smiled back gratefully, before slipping through the door and back to the party.

'What do we do now?' Tiko asked after a moment. 'We still haven't found the presents.'

'We've searched everywhere inside the palace and its grounds,' Aziza said. 'But what about outside. Like outside, outside.'

'Actually . . .' Peri began, an excited look on her face. 'That's not quite true. We haven't searched the royal vaults.'

Aziza frowned. 'The vaults?'

'They're deep beneath the palace,' Tiko offered.

Peri nodded. 'If I wanted to hide something, that's where I'd put it.'

But wouldn't the vaults be hard to get into? Aziza wondered. *And why would someone put presents in the vault?* One look at Peri's determined face and Aziza shrugged. *Peri knows the palace better than anyone. And in Shimmerton things aren't always as they seem!*

Peri suddenly gasped as she spotted the time on a nearby clock. 'I'm such a terrible host. I've barely been at my own party.'

Tiko patted her arm. 'It's going to be OK. Why don't I go check that everything is running smoothly? I'll tell your parents that you'll be back very soon.' Tiko began patting himself down. 'I just need to find my clipboard.' He scurried off.

'It's not fair,' Peri sighed. 'I wish we could all just be at the party together. I wish we didn't even have to look for those presents.' She bit her lip. 'I know I was nervous about the party going perfectly, but I was really looking forward to it too and now everything is ruined.'

Aziza gave her a quick hug. 'Don't worry. The sooner we find those gifts, the sooner we can get back to the party!'

Chapter 5

The rickety wooden staircase creaked an unhappy sound as Peri and Aziza descended slowly into the depths of the palace. The space was narrow, dark and a little creepy.

'Nearly there,' Peri called back cheerfully.

How is she not scared? Aziza wondered with a shiver. *I hate basements.*

Cobwebs decorated the stone walls and, even with the glowing torches in the wall sconces, darkness danced around them. At last, they reached the bottom and Aziza could see a sturdy wooden door.

'I hope you have the key,' Aziza whispered, eager to leave the stairway.

'Not a key exactly,' Peri replied with a secretive smile. Then she stepped closer to the door and whispered a single word. 'Shimmerton!'

Immediately the wall began to glow, then, with a heavy groan, the door swung open.

Glittersticks, a magical password! Aziza realized. *It's not very difficult though. Who is in charge of security around this place?*

The two girls entered the vault, their footsteps echoing loudly. It was huge and filled with treasure chests, battle armour and ball gowns of silk, lace and velvet hanging from wooden rails. Lanterns dangled from the walls, casting an eerie glow over everything.

Then there was the golden carriage that sat in the middle of the vault. The sides of it were decorated with beautiful paintings of fairies granting wishes. Even its massive wheels were covered in gold. It looked like something Cinderella would have travelled in.

Aziza moved closer to the carriage, unable to believe what she was seeing.

'This vault is where Mum and Dad keep

all their old royal stuff,' Peri said, following her. 'Dad likes to collect historical artefacts, but Mum made him move the carriage down here because it was cluttering up the palace.'

'It's like being in a museum,' Aziza said, unable to take her eyes off the carriage. She ran a hand along a gleaming door.

Smiling, Peri opened it. 'You can sit in it if you want. Dad hasn't used it since he upgraded to a Caspian3000 model.'

Aziza climbed into the carriage. The plush velvet seat sank gently under her weight. *It's like sitting on a cloud.* Aziza felt like a princess on her way to some important event. She closed her eyes, imagining the crowd of people cheering as she moved past, waving.

The sudden sound of footsteps startled Aziza and her eyes flew open. She realized with a start that she was *actually* waving . . . also, Peri had disappeared!

Aziza scrambled out of the carriage, feeling a bit embarrassed. She looked around for Peri, but couldn't see her anywhere. *I don't want to be stuck here alone*, she thought, a bit worried. *It's not actually that scary, but still.*

Hurrying past the carriage, Aziza found Peri looking inside a golden chest. Next to it were several more and it looked like Peri had already been through them. There were things scattered on the ground close by.

We're wasting time, Aziza thought. *Why would someone hide the presents down here?*

'Um, Peri, do you really think they're going to be here?' Aziza asked.

Peri was still rummaging through the chest.

'What?' Her voice was muffled.

'Why would someone take presents, just to hide them here?' Aziza tried again. 'It doesn't make sense. I think we should be looking outside the palace.'

Peri stood up quickly, a frown on her face. 'We don't know why the presents were taken so we need to check everywhere in the palace first.' She placed her hands on her hips. 'I *do* know what I'm doing.'

'So do I,' Aziza said. 'I helped find Ccoa the Ice Cat, remember?'

Peri's eyebrows shot up. 'I was there too,

you know. You didn't do it alone.'

'Look. I'm just trying to help,' Aziza finally burst out. 'Being here isn't going to help.'

Peri crossed her arms. 'Well just go then. If that's what you really want.' Peri's voice was a bit squeaky.

Aziza could feel her face getting hot and her throat felt tight. 'Fine. Happy Birthday, Peri.' She shook her head. 'All I wanted to do was help.'

'I'm so sorry, Aziza,' Peri whispered quietly. 'I didn't mean it. I know you're just trying to help.'

Peri looked so miserable that Aziza couldn't stay mad at her any more. Aziza remembered how frustrated she'd felt just before coming to Shimmerton. How she'd snapped at Otis.

'It's OK,' she said quietly. 'I know how you feel.'

Peri's eyes filled with tears. 'I'm just so stressed about finding the presents.'

Aziza nodded and gave Peri a quick hug. 'Let's keep looking,' she said, glancing around. 'What about over there?' she added and pointed to a large glass cupboard full of tiny statues and other objects like bejewelled bottles and ornately decorated pens.

Together they made their way to the cupboard and began to search. Neither spoke, still feeling a bit awkward.

Peri held up a silver tiara. 'I forgot all about this,' she exclaimed. At Aziza's puzzled look, Peri placed the tiara atop of Aziza's coily strands. 'It's my spare tiara.'

Both girls grinned at each other for a moment then got back to searching. Then a strange shimmer caught Aziza's attention and she pulled out a spool of yellow ribbon. It was glowing!

'Magic ribbon,' Peri told her and pulled out two more spools from the cupboard, each one a different colour. 'I used this stuff to wrap some of the presents.'

Aziza turned the spool over, marvelling at the way it shimmered. 'It's so pretty.'

'It's the pixie dust,' Peri said, replacing each spool of ribbon carefully. 'The dust

inspires joy and

creativity.

That's why

the ribbons

are so

precious.'

They continued

searching the vaults looking under the row

of dresses and even the suits of armour. They

searched every inch of the vault, but the

presents were nowhere to be found.

'That's it,' Peri finally sighed. 'I'm totally

getting bad luck for the rest of the year.'

'What do you mean?' Aziza asked.

'If I don't give out any presents on my birthday, I kind of get bad luck for 365 days.'

'No way!' Aziza gasped.

'It's a Shimmerton thing. People don't talk about it so much and it is only a smidgin of bad luck.' Peri's shoulders dropped. 'The worst thing is that I'll have let my parents down.'

'You sound like you're giving up!' Aziza exclaimed. 'And you never give up. Remember the first time we met and you told me that we'd find the Gigglers and get my doorknob back? Or when you taught me how to fly?'

'You're right,' Peri said, a determined look slipping over her face. 'I did do that.'

Aziza grinned. 'Some lost birthday presents aren't going to defeat us!'

Chapter 6

Aziza and Peri quickly made their way back to the grand ballroom where the guests had now gathered once more. The party was in full swing. Tiko was talking to Mrs Hattie and Finn Bracken had taken over the DJing and was playing all the latest Shimmerton hits. Even the king and queen were dancing up a storm on the dance floor. Peri gaped as her dad twirled her mum around before dipping her over his arm.

At least the party is going well, Aziza thought cheerfully as they made their way over to Tiko.

'Peri, Aziza!' Tiko exclaimed when he caught sight of them. 'I'm so glad you're back. We found the presents. Mrs Hattie just told me.'

The girls stared at each other in shock.

'You did?' Aziza finally replied. 'Where?'

'Mrs Hattie said the staff were moving the presents around to keep them safe.' Tiko pointed over to a table that was now piled high with brightly wrapped parcels. 'She tracked them all down.'

Relieved, Peri peered over the table intently, but then she frowned and shook her head.

'What's the matter?' Tiko said confused. 'I thought you'd be happy.'

'That's most of the presents,' she cried. 'But there are still three missing.' She turned to Aziza with a worried look. 'The ones I wrapped with magical ribbons.'

Aziza nodded in understanding. She knew how important those presents were to Peri.

'We'll find them,' she assured her with a quick squeeze.

Peri looked up at the big clock in the ballroom. 'But it's almost time to give them out. And I really wanted my mum to get her lavender oil and lotion. She's all out of the stuff and it's her fave.'

'Lavender?' Suddenly Tiko's nose started twitching. 'Hang on! I can smell that.'

'It must be Mum's lotion!' Peri squealed.

'Can you follow the scent?' Aziza asked. 'It might lead us to the missing presents.'

Tiko took a deep breath, his nose twitching frantically. 'I've got this.'

Together, Aziza and Peri followed Tiko's

nose out of the ballroom, through the golden hallway, past the spiral staircase and back outside. Tiko sniffed again and instead of heading for the glasshouse, he led them towards the palace gate and past the startled toy guards. Soon they'd left the palace grounds entirely. They continued until they reached a little, grassy lane, just off the paved driveway.

'I can smell it as well now,' Aziza cried, sniffing the air.

'Me too,' Peri said. 'And can you hear that?'

'It sounds like music,' Tiko replied.

'It's the tune from the music box I got my dad,' Peri explained. She was practically hopping on the spot with excitement. 'We must be close.'

The friends turned off onto the lane and followed the sound until they reached a tall hedge. In front of it was a huge tree with thick branches and even thicker leaves that were spread out like a giant hand.

It's a Handy tree, Aziza realized. She'd seen one on her last visit to Shimmerton. But the music seemed to be coming from its trunk. *That's so strange. I didn't know Handy trees made music.*

'Look,' Tiko called out, pointing to the base of the tree.

Sure enough, lying beneath the protective cover of the Handy tree's leaves were the three small parcels. One was lavender, one orange and the other yellow.

'My presents,' Peri cried and dashed towards them.

Tiko sniffed the air again. 'I wonder who left them here.'

Aziza wondered the same thing, but then something even more puzzling caught her attention.

'It doesn't matter any more.' Peri gathered the presents into her arms. 'I'm just glad we found them.'

'But Peri,' Aziza said. 'The ribbons are missing.'

'Whaaat?' Peri screeched and turned the

presents over. 'Where are they?'

That's so weird, Aziza thought. *Why would someone leave the presents, but take the ribbons?* Just then Aziza heard a strange sound. It sounded like someone was . . . sniffling?

With a frantic motion, Aziza waved at her friends to be quiet.

Everything went silent then a muffled voice snapped.

'Gah! Get off.' More silence then. 'Stop sticking to me!'

Aziza looked at her two friends and Tiko pointed. The sound was coming from the other side of the hedge. *But who could it be?*

The friends moved closer to the hedge and Aziza spied a small gap, just big enough to look through. She peered through it to find a girl in a brightly coloured dress. Her rainbow-coloured braids swung about as she hopped from one foot to the other. *What an odd little dance*, Aziza thought.

'It's Resa,' Aziza whispered as she turned back to her friends. 'She's dancing though.'

'You don't think she's got anything to do with the missing ribbons, do you?' Tiko said with a worried look. 'I don't believe she would steal them?'

'We need to get to the other side and find out.' Peri looked determined.

'How are we going to do that?' Tiko cried, staring up at the high hedge.

'You're going to shapeshift, Tiko, and me and Aziza are going to fly.' Peri turned to Aziza. 'Think you can find a happy thought?'

'You know it!' Aziza replied. It was the happiness that would help her float.

Tiko shut his eyes, scrunched up his nose again and disappeared. This time when he reappeared, he was a tiny mouse. Just small enough to squeeze through the hole.

'Nice one, Tiko,' Peri cried as she zoomed up into the air. 'Meet you on the other side.'

He's definitely getting better at shapeshifting, Aziza thought as Tiko scurried out of sight. Then with her happy thought in place, she flew up behind Peri. The feel of the air rushing past her face felt amazing. *I've missed this.*

It took them no time to fly across the hedge and when they landed on the other

side they found Tiko waiting, back to his usual self. Resa still had her back to them and was hopping about still doing her funny little dance.

'Ahem,' Peri coughed.

Resa whirled around, arms lifted and a shocked look on her face. Dangling from her hands were three shimmering ribbons. Resa took one look at Aziza and her friends and . . . burst into tears.

Chapter 7

'It's not what it looks like,' Resa sobbed. 'I promise.'

Peri marched right up to her. 'It looks like you took my presents and my ribbons.'

Resa swallowed hard. 'I didn't mean

to. I overhead you guys with the unicorn, talking about how the ribbons inspire joy and creativity—'

'You were eavesdropping too?' Peri interrupted in an indignant voice.

'No . . . I mean yes,' Resa rubbed her forehead, and the ribbons flapped in the air. 'I'm not making any sense.'

Aziza stepped forward and placed a hand on Peri's arm. 'Why don't we just let her explain?'

For a second, it looked like Peri might argue, but then she took a deep breath and nodded.

'Go on, Resa,' Aziza said gently.

'I saw the presents in the ballroom and I only meant to touch the ribbons, truly. I was hoping it would cheer me up and bring back my rainbow.' Resa lifted her hands. 'But the ribbons curled up my arms all by themselves. Now they're stuck like glue and I can't get them off.'

So that's what she was talking about when she said get off, Aziza realized. *And why she was doing that funny dance.*

'I didn't want anyone to know what happened,' Resa continued. 'It's totally embarrassing. So, I snuck out with the ribbons and the presents while everyone was dancing. I managed to get the ribbons off the presents but they won't come off *me* and I don't know what to do!' Resa ended on a wail.

'They're covered in pixie dust,' Peri said in a softer voice. 'You can never tell what those ribbons will do.' She looked thoughtful for a moment. 'My mum says there's always a reason though, when they behave funny.'

Resa was crying again, runny nose and everything. 'Everyone's going to think I'm a thief. That's why I couldn't return the presents to the palace.'

Tiko stepped forward and handed her a tissue. Resa took it and blew her nose with a noisy toot.

'I put them under the Handy tree because I knew they'd be safe there, and that's when you guys showed up.'

So that's what happened to the presents, Aziza

thought. But something still didn't make sense to her.

'What did you mean about bringing back your rainbow?' Aziza asked Resa.

'I'm the newest Rainbow Maker for Shimmerton,' Resa explained. 'But my rainbow colours keep fading. I've been trying to fix it and I thought the ribbons might help inspire me but it didn't work – look!'

Resa raised her arms and the ends of the ribbons flapped wildly. Aziza, Tiko and Peri looked up, but nothing happened for a moment. Then suddenly, a wonky

washed-out rainbow appeared in the sky.

'See,' Resa cried, 'it's all faded.'

Aziza did see and when she looked at Resa again, she realized something else. *She looks a bit faded too. Her hair isn't as bright as it used to be.*

'When did your rainbows start fading?' Peri asked.

Resa thought for a moment. 'I think it was a week ago.'

'Did anything unusual happen then?' Aziza said. 'There must be a reason or clue.'

'I don't think so. I remember someone

making fun of my wonky rainbows.' Resa looked away. 'I know my rainbows aren't perfect, but I'm trying my best.'

Peri gasped. 'That's not very nice. I hope you told a grown-up. My mum says you should always speak up when people are being mean.'

Resa just stared at her. 'Oh no, I couldn't. I'm so new at being a Rainbow Maker.'

'So, what did you do?' Tiko asked.

Resa's chin dropped. 'I just stopped making my rainbows in front of people. But then they started to lose their colour and that's way worse than a wonky rainbow.'

Even as she spoke, Resa looked duller and duller. She was fading even more.

'I so wanted to be the youngest ever Rainbow Maker for Shimmerton,' Resa added. 'But now I wish I'd never been chosen. It's too much responsibility and I hate it.'

Aziza noticed then that Tiko was being awfully quiet. In fact, he looked like he was trying to figure something out.

'Tiko?' Aziza said.

Tiko tapped his chin. 'Maybe it's not creativity you're missing,' he said to Resa.

'Maybe you need to get your confidence back. It sounds like your rainbows started to fade when you lost your confidence.' Tiko scratched his head. 'It's just an idea though.'

'It's a brilliant idea, Tiko.' Peri replied. 'But

the only way to know for sure is for Resa to get her confidence back.'

Resa perked up a bit. 'How?'

Peri shrugged. 'I'm not actually sure. It's not really something you turn off and on, is it?'

Resa's face dropped again and Aziza remembered a trick her parents used when they were working on a Jamal Justice graphic novel. Sometimes when one of them thought their writing or their illustrations were rubbish, the other one would tell them all the things they liked about them. *Maybe it'll help*

Resa feel better, Aziza thought.

Aziza told her friends her idea. 'It always seems to work with my mum and dad.'

Resa looked doubtful.

'I'll go first,' Aziza said. 'I think your erm . . .' Aziza's voice trailed off as she struggled to think of something.

Resa started to cry again. 'I don't think this is going to work.'

'Only because we don't know you that well.' Aziza replied quickly. 'I know . . . I like your honesty. You didn't lie when we found you with the ribbons and you didn't run away. That was super cool.'

'Yeah,' Peri said. 'And you're proper gentle too. You got those ribbons off without messing up my presents and you kept them safe.'

Resa smiled, it was a small one, but a smile, nonetheless.

'I really like your hair,' Tiko piped up. 'It's super pretty and very neat.' He stroked a hand over his head. 'Just like my hairstyle.'

That made all of them laugh!

After that, the compliments came much

easier and Resa's smile grew bigger with each kind word.

'What do you like about yourself?' Aziza asked Resa suddenly.

Resa's smile dipped a bit and she ducked her head. 'Isn't it a bit big-headed to say what you like about yourself?' Resa asked.

'Absolutely not,' Aziza said. 'My mum gets me to tell her every day something I love about myself.'

Resa cocked her head to one side. 'OK, I'm listening.'

Aziza thought about Peri and Tiko and all their adventures. She thought of Otis and the party she was planning for him.

'I like that I'm a good friend and sister,' Aziza said with pride.

Peri nodded with enthusiasm. 'I like that I'm funny.'

Tiko rolled his eyes.

'What? I am!' Peri insisted.

'What about you, Tiko?' Resa asked softly.

Tiko thought for a minute and then a big grin spread over his face. 'I like that I can shapeshift and that I'm getting better every time I try.'

Resa grinned back and took a deep breath. 'I like that I'm really determined and I always try my best.'

'See!' Aziza said. 'It's easy when you try.'

Peri gave Resa a high five.

'Do you think you could try that rainbow

again?' Aziza asked her.

'Promise you won't laugh if it's rubbish?'

'We promise,' Peri, Tiko and Aziza said at the same time.

So Resa lifted her arms in the air again and Aziza held her breath as she waited to see what would happen.

Chapter 8

Almost immediately a rainbow began to form. The colours wriggled across the sky, faint at first, but then they got stronger. Until eventually a fully formed rainbow shone brightly above them.

'It's beautiful,' Aziza breathed.

Resa frowned. 'It's wonky.'

'It's unique,' Peri said firmly.

'And you tried your best,' Tiko added. 'That's what matters most.'

Resa stared at her rainbow again and smiled a wonky smile. 'It is beautiful and it is unique and I did try my best.' She nodded in satisfaction and almost immediately, the ribbons fell away from her arms and hands. Tiko dived forward to catch them before they landed on the ground.

'I'm ribbonless,' Resa cried, waving her

hands about in relief. 'Goodness, that feels good.'

'Nice catch,' Peri said as Tiko handed the shimmering ribbons back to her.

Resa turned to Aziza and her friends. 'Thank you so much. I should have just told someone when my rainbows started to fade. I'd worked so hard to become the youngest Rainbow Maker that I didn't want to ask for help.'

Peri made a face. 'I know what you mean. It's really hard being a princess, and everyone expects me to be perfect.' Then she scrunched up her nose. 'And to stay clean and tidy.'

'You do find that really hard,' Tiko said.

Peri grinned. 'You have no idea.' She lifted a lavender ribbon. 'I've spent the whole day looking for missing presents and ended up missing my own birthday party. I should have just told my parents what was going on and asked for help.'

'*The smartest people ask for help.*' Aziza remembered her dad's words. She shifted in place as she remembered her parents' offer to help with Otis's party.

'I've been planning my brother's surprise birthday party back home,' she confessed. 'I wanted it to be perfect and gave myself too many things to do at the same time.'

Peri took Aziza's hand. 'I wish you'd said something. All this time we've been so caught up in my problems.'

'It's OK,' Aziza replied. 'Today has shown me what's important. I know Otis will love the party no matter how it turns out because he'll know I did my best.'

Tiko coughed and Peri and Aziza turned to him. 'I might have been struggling organizing Peri's party. I didn't say anything because I didn't want to let you down.'

'Oh Tiko,' Peri breathed. She hugged him 'You know you could never let me down.'

'I do now. But it definitely feels better to talk about it.'

All four friends looked at each other and then burst out laughing. 'All of our problems had a really simple answer,' Aziza said. 'Come on, it's time for a party.'

Tiko pulled out his clipboard from a hidden place in his fur.

After collecting the presents and reattaching the ribbons, the four friends made their way back to the ballroom. Just as they passed

the staircase, Resa stopped suddenly.

'I'll catch up with you guys,' she said. 'I've got something to take care of.'

Then she darted off towards the kitchens.

Peri stared after her. 'What was that about?'

Aziza and Tiko shrugged and the trio continued to the ballroom hall. The party was still in full swing and the dance floor was filled with happy creatures.

'Peri, darling,' the queen cried rushing over to them. 'Where have you been?'

The king was right behind her. 'We were getting worried.'

'Erm . . . about that,' Peri began and she told her parents all about the missing presents. 'I'm so sorry,' she finished. 'I just didn't want to let you down.'

The king took Peri by the shoulders. 'We know being a princess is difficult. With all the boring meetings and stuffy clothes, but we really just want you to be happy.'

The queen took her hand. 'You know you can always come to us if you have a problem.'

Peri sniffed and nodded, just as Mrs Hattie bustled into the hall with Resa at her side. She was pushing a trolley and on top of it sat an enormous cake. Eight tiers of brightly frosted sponge cake towered over everyone.

Glittersticks! Aziza couldn't stop staring at it. *It looks like it's made out of rainbows.*

'Did you do that?' Peri breathed.

Resa nodded. 'I wanted to say thank you for helping and believing in me.'

Mrs Hattie wheeled the cake in front of Peri. 'Come on, your Highness, it's time to cut the cake.'

'Don't forget to make a wish,' Tiko reminded her quickly.

Peri closed her eyes tightly and took a deep breath. The room went silent as the princess made her special birthday wish. Then Peri opened her eyes and a wide smile lit up her face.

I wonder what it is, Aziza thought. But she didn't ask Peri – for everyone knows wishes won't come true if you reveal them.

Then it was time to hand out the gifts and Aziza stepped back as all of the guests crowded around the royal family. She didn't even live in Shimmerton so knew she wouldn't have a gift.

There were so many gifts. From the matching rapping tambourines for Finn and Fern, to a bag of the tastiest bird seed for Mrs Hattie. Nansi loved his eight socks and even

the Gigglers seemed
pleased with their
sparkly toy wands.
Then it came time for
the most special gifts of all. Peri's parents were

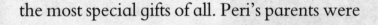

delighted with
the lavender
toiletries
and musical
box.

'This is for
you,' Peri said, handing Tiko his gift. 'I
wasn't sure what you'd like.'

Tiko ripped through the wrapping paper to find a blue and gold pen. He looked up in confusion.

'It's a forget-me-not pen,' Peri said quickly. 'It magically writes down the things you've forgotten so you never miss anything.'

Tiko's mouth dropped open, and his eyes went a bit shiny.

Peri's face dropped. 'Don't you like it?'

'I love it!' Tiko cried.

Peri smiled in relief. She began to scan the crowd of guests. 'Where's Aziza? I need to give her a present.'

'Me?' Aziza squeaked. She pushed through the happy guests, busy playing with their gifts. 'You didn't even know I was coming.'

'I hoped the fairy door would do its thing so I got this ready, just in case.'

Peri opened her hand and inside was a friendship bracelet. But

not just any ordinary one – this bracelet shimmered with pixie dust!

'You made it with the magic ribbons,' Aziza gasped as she picked it up.

Peri nodded with a grin as Aziza tied it around her wrist.

'I'll never take it off!' Aziza promised and gave her a hug.

'Careful,' Tiko teased. 'The ribbons just might hear you and decide to stay on for ever.'

'Come on,' Peri cried. 'We solved the mystery of the missing presents. Now it's time to party!'

And so, they did. They played extra party

games and Kendra wasn't too happy when Aziza beat her at pin the tail on the dragon. They tried all the food items on the menu, finishing with the rainbow cake that tasted like . . . well a rainbow . . . obviously. Aziza even learned the dance to Shimmerton's most popular song 'Who Let the Elves Out'. But soon it was time for Aziza to return home.

'Do you think you'll be all right organizing Otis's party?' Peri asked as they stood in front of the glowing fairy door.

'I could lend you my pen if you want,' Tiko added.

'Thanks, but I'll be fine,' Aziza replied. 'I'm going to ask my parents for help.'

Aziza hugged her friends goodbye and as she stepped through the door she realized she wasn't worried any more. Now she knew how important it was to ask for help, everything truly would be fine.

Myths and Legends

Aziza, her friends, and the inhabitants of Shimmerton are inspired by myths and legends from all around the world:

Aziza is named after a type of fairy creature. In West African folklore, specifically *Dahomey mythology*, the Aziza are helpful fairies who live in the forest and are full of wisdom.

Peri's name comes from ancient Persian mythology. Peris are winged spirits who can be kind and helpful, but they also sometimes enjoy playing tricks on people. In paintings they are usually shown with large, bird-like wings.

Resa is based on a South African deity called Mbaba Mwana Waresa. She rules over harvests, agriculture, rain and – of course – rainbows.

Nansi is named after Anansi, a mischievous trickster from West African mythology. He appears most often in Ghanaian folklore and can take many different forms, but most often he takes the shape of a spider.

Unicorns, like Mr Bracken, Fern and Finn, have appeared in folklore for thousands of years. They're normally portrayed as magical, horned white horses and are said to have healing powers.

Ccoa comes from Peruvian folklore. The ccoa is a cat-like creature and the companion of a mountain god. It can bring about storms, hail and lightning. Find out more about Ccoa in *Aziza's Secret Fairy Door and the Ice Cat Mystery*.

Mrs Sayeed's son is an **Almiraj**, a legendary rabbit with a unicorn-like horn. They are found in Arabic myths and folklore.

Brownies are part of Scottish folklore. They are very helpful creatures that do lots of chores around the house.

Pixies are mythological creatures from English folktales. They are tiny, magical creatures – a bit like fairies – but they don't have wings.

Mrs Hattie is a **sphinx**. In Greek and ancient Egyptian mythology, the sphinx is a mythical creature with a human head, a lion's body and large bird wings.

Join Aziza on her brand new
magical adventure in

Coming in June 2022

Chapter 1

The relentless sound of heavy rain beating against the window echoed across the living room. Aziza stared glumly at the big fat droplets sliding down the fogged-up glass. *It's supposed to be summer*, she thought.

'Has anyone seen the tent?' bellowed Dad from the hallway. 'I need to get it in the car first, so we can see how much space we have left for the rest of the camping stuff.'

Aziza poked her head into the corridor. She could only see half of her dad. The other half was deep inside a cupboard. He was surrounded by boxes of the Jamal Justice graphic novels that Aziza's mum and dad wrote. Jamal Justice was a really popular character, and the books took up loads of space in the flat.

'Nope, no tent!' hollered Otis, as he leapt

over the boxes of books and then dodged past the piles of camping gear to finally get into the living room. He flopped down on the sofa. 'I did find my rucksack, though, and look.' He held up a greyish looking square and waved it at Aziza. 'I even found a piece of chocolate from last year's trip.'

Otis popped the prize into his mouth.

'Eww,' Aziza squealed at her brother.

'Otis, what have I told you about eating unidentifiable objects?' Mum said with a frown as she entered from the kitchen.

'Sorry, Mum,' Otis said with a chocolatey

 3

grin. 'I need to keep my energy up if we're going camping.'

Mum's frown deepened. 'Camping,' she muttered. 'When I married your father, I said for better or worse. He didn't say anything about camping.'

'Come on, honey,' Dad said, striding into the room. A long, red bag was cradled in his arms. 'I've found the tent now. It's all good.'

Mum raised a doubtful eyebrow. 'Good? Have you seen the weather?'

'I'm sure it will get better,' Aziza piped up.

Mum sighed and looked longingly at the

glossy holiday magazine on the side table. She picked it up and waved it in the air.

'Just look at this: sun, sea and sand,' she said longingly. 'It would have been simply superb.'

Dad grabbed the magazine, a wide grin splitting his face. 'Superb kindling for a fire, you mean.'

'We'll need a fire!' Mum replied with a snort. 'It's freezing out there.'

Dad laughed and Aziza watched as Mum playfully tried to retrieve the magazine. Aziza had been really looking forward to the trip.

They had tried camping for the first time last year and it had been great. But it had also been dry. *Are we going to be stuck in that tiny tent together for a whole week? I'd better take some books with me.*

'I'm going to finish packing,' Aziza said, leaving her parents and Otis behind and heading to her room.

Resting on her sparkly Fairy Power duvet was Aziza's half-filled rucksack. Aziza looked round her room to find the latest Fairy Power book. She froze as she spotted a thin trail of golden sand and tiny seashells dusting her windowsill and leading past Lil, her pot plant, and right up to the . . . secret fairy door.

Small fragments of smooth sea glass were studded into the door, making it sparkle like a coloured mosaic. The door stood slightly ajar as if it were inviting Aziza to go through. She shivered with excitement. *It's time to go back to the magical kingdom of Shimmerton!* Aziza hesitated for a moment and glanced back at her rucksack. *But what about the holiday?* Then she remembered. Time moved faster in Shimmerton. *I'll be back before Dad has even put that tent in the car!*

Aziza touched the sparkly doorknob and immediately she felt herself start to shrink. This time she didn't hesitate, and she ran straight through the fairy door. Bright sunshine greeted her on the other side and Aziza blinked in wonder at the sandy beach stretching out in front of her, leading towards a deep blue sea.

The sun blazed down from a cloudless pink sky, warming her bare shoulders. Aziza looked down to find her jeans and T-shirt were gone, replaced by a cute playsuit that matched the colours of her butterfly wings.

Wow. Aziza did a small spin. She could feel the wings fluttering behind her. *I'm definitely not home any more.* The fairy door was shut tight again. Its edges blended invisibly into the trunk of a large palm tree. If you didn't know it was there, you wouldn't notice it.

Just then a beach ball bounced past Aziza and a small Almiraj sprinted after it. His long bunny ears trailed in the wind behind him. In fact, the beach was packed full of Shimmerton residents having fun. Music filled the air, and the leaves of the palm trees seemed to sway in time to the beat. At the edge of the beach was a huge barbecue. The pharmacist Mr Phoenix stood next to it. Flames burst from his bright red feathers keeping the grill hot, while two ogres chatted as they waited in line to be served their halloumi kebabs.

In the water was Neith the weaver. She was whizzing along on a giant inflatable potato. Golden sparkles seemed to cover her and Aziza realized that the inflatable must be powered by some kind of magic. *It feels like carnival weekend*, Aziza thought, looking at everybody's smiling faces as they ate and danced and laughed with each other.

But where are Tiko and Peri? Aziza searched through the crowd, trying to find her friends.

'You're having a laugh!' an outraged voice suddenly protested. 'Our castle is not a hazard.'

Aziza stood on tiptoe and spotted Kendra, Noon and Felly standing by a very tall sandcastle. It had turrets and *even* balconies. Kendra was busy waving a sand-covered shovel in the air as she spoke.

'It's totally epic,' Noon agreed, dodging flying sand.

'And we totally didn't move anyone's

chair, picnic blanket or swimming trunks to make space,' Felly added.

Kendra rolled her eyes, and Noon elbowed Felly sharply.

'What?' Felly grumbled, rubbing her side.

Ugh, of course the Gigglers are here and making a drama as usual, Aziza thought.

'Young ladies, sandcastles must adhere to strict size limits.' Officer Alf appeared from the other side of the sandcastle. He had his elf and safety clipboard in one hand and a tape measure in the other. 'You cannot just go moving sand around.'

'Why not?' Noon asked.

Officer Alf sighed. 'Because—'

'You're just jealous,' Kendra interrupted with a roll of her eyes. 'Because we're the queens of the beach.'

The Elf and Safety Officer's mouth dropped open in shock and the three fairies giggled. He then jabbed at some notes on his clipboard and started to tell them that all this digging was very disruptive and . . .

Aziza gasped as she spotted a small bear-like creature just a few metres away by the seashore. It was her friend Tiko! *And look, there's Peri too*, Aziza thought as she started to run towards the fairy princess with swan-like wings.

As Aziza got closer, she realized that Peri and Tiko were trying to skim stones across the water and they weren't alone. Next to them, sitting on a rock that was being lapped by the waves was a pretty girl with the longest locks Aziza had ever seen. In her hand was a stone and, as she threw it, it danced perfectly across the waves until it disappeared out of sight.

'*I wonder who she . . .*' but the thought was

left unfinished as she realized something amazing. *'Glittersticks!'* Aziza breathed. The new girl was a mermaid. An actual mermaid!

About the Authors

Lola Morayo is the pen name for the creative partnership of writers Tọ́lá Okogwu and Jasmine Richards.

© Dujonna Gift-Simms

Tọ́lá is a journalist and author of the Daddy Do My Hair series. She is an avid reader who enjoys spending time with her family and friends in her home in Kent, where she lives with her husband and daughters.

Jasmine is the founder of an inclusive fiction studio called Storymix and has written more than fifteen books for children. She lives in Hertfordshire with her husband and two children.

Both are passionate about telling stories that are inclusive and joyful.

About the Illustrator

© Katarina Tibenska

Cory Reid lives in Kettering and is an illustrator and designer who has worked in the creative industry for more than fifteen years, with clients including Usborne Publishing, Owlet Press and Card Factory.